MY EARL, THE SPY

THE TRENGROUSE BALL
BOOK FIVE

ELIZABETH LEYDIN

IMPROBABLE FICTIONS

Improbable Fictions
PO Box 283
Annandale NSW 2038
Australia
contact@improbablefictions.com

THE TRENGROUSE BALL

The Trengrouse Ball…one magic night in a Cornish summer. Music, dancing, flirting and laughter. And deception, abduction, love and loss. New attractions, new hopes, and old flames rekindled. For some, a culmination. For others, a new beginning.

The Trengrouse Ball series follows the lives and loves of the Trengrouse family: eight grown children of the Earl of Trengrouse, each of whom is searching for the life they need; each battling their own fears but hoping for happy ever after.

After the Trengrouse Ball, their lives will never be the same again…

CHAPTER 1

JULY, 1815

Charles Goddard, Earl of Westholm, ran up the steps at Whitehall and made his way to Lord Castlereagh's office.

It was guarded, as always, by his secretary: a sharp-faced middle-aged man named Boniface, who was better than a troop of dragoons at keeping unwanted visitors away from the Foreign Secretary.

Boniface nodded and waved Charles through; a rare honour, and significant.

Castlereagh must be anxious about this latest dispatch. Scovell, his lordship's top code-breaker, was still in Belgium, so this message must have come through their agents somewhere else. Thus the need for Charles and his 'ciphering genius friend'.

Castlereagh was, as always, going through papers at his desk, dressed impeccably despite the heat and the smell rising from the Thames. July in London was unpleasant, even in the seat of power.

He rose to shake Charles' hand. His lordship was a harsh man to those he considered beneath him, especially the working class, but Charles, being a peer himself, was always accorded correct etiquette, despite being impoverished enough to need an actual job in government. Charles wasn't *quite* cynical enough to think that was only because he had a vote in the House of Lords, and was thus useful to the government in getting bills passed.

"We have a new intercepted message," Castlereagh said, "and my lot can't make head nor tale of it. *I think it's in Russian. But it was intercepted *here*, in London."

"Did it come via the Russians?"

"No. Via a new courier, an importer of lace. You know, the market for French lace has ballooned since peace was declared."

Yes indeed. Imports of French lace and brandy and other items had been illegal for more than a decade, since Britain and France had last been at peace. The *ton* still *wore* French lace, of course, bought from smugglers or at astronomical prices from Swiss middlemen.

"Why think it's Russian, then?"

"They've been up to something. Stalling the peace negotiations. Could be the French, of course. They're agitating about the occupation, threatening resumption of hostilities. I'm leaving on Friday for Paris to push the treaty along, and I want to know what's in that dispatch by then."

Since Waterloo and Napoleon's arrest, the major powers had been locked in treaty talks in Paris. They weren't going well.

"How did it come?"

"Our man managed to copy it while the courier was knocked out by drinking too much free brandy." Castlereagh shrugged and gave a *moue* of distaste. His lordship accepted the less honorable elements of espionage, but he didn't like them.

"Addressed to?" Charles asked.

"No address. The courier delivered it to a warehouse. Obviously a meeting—but it had so many people coming and going from it that day that it could have ended up anywhere."

"So we need to break it."

Castlereagh nodded. "We need to break it." He handed over a heavily sealed packet of papers. "Can you get your fellow onto it?"

"Yes, but he's in the country for the summer. It may take a day or two."

"Fast as you can. Meet me Friday at Dover if you can't get it before then. You yourself, mind, not a courier. I *need* to know who in London has been having secret correspondence with—well, either our enemies or our supposed friends. I've lived long enough to know that wartime alliances break apart rapidly once peace comes. We can't trust any of them."

Perhaps not even their own people. It was disturbing.

"You think it's this Augustine?"

"It could be. I *would* like to know who he is."

Augustine was a name their agents had heard in the wrong circles: supposedly, an English traitor high up in the government. These things were usually exaggerated, though. Probably no more than a lowly clerk.

Castlereagh picked up his pen in dismissal, and then paused. "It's deuced odd that this fellow of yours doesn't want pay. Are you sure he can be trusted?"

Charles grinned. He'd worked hard to keep his code-breaker's identity secret, declaring that, without that, no code-breaking or inventions of new ciphers would happen. "My fellow is the child of a British peer. As loyal to the Crown as you or I. And definitely not in need of pay."

Castlereagh let out a sigh, and relaxed. Charles could just about hear him think, *Ah, one of us chaps*. If only he knew.

"Well, then. Off you go."

As he headed down the steps towards St James's, Charles felt his heart grow light. Out of the city, on government business.

If he rode, he'd be with Melissa by tomorrow.

THE WONDERFUL THING about being a lady of quality was that one didn't have to understand why people said the things they did— one just had to know the approved response. It was a great comfort.

Melissa Trengrouse nodded as her sister Kerenza's best friend, Katie Kelynack, said, "Isn't it exciting? I'm so looking forward to this ball!"

"Oh, so am I!" Kerenza agreed. "I wish it were tomorrow, instead of next month!"

Why anyone would look forward to a ball was beyond Melissa, but Katie and Kerenza had been in what her mother called 'a tizzy' about it for months.

The three of them were arranging flowers; an occupation Mama thought of as ladylike. Melissa was aware she had a reputation for always producing beautiful centrepieces; it was easy enough, if you just followed the Golden Mean. Art was so often about mathematics.

"It will be a big affair," Melissa said. There. That remark was unexceptional. Sure enough, it sent Katie and Kerenza into a litany of who was coming, who *wouldn't* be coming and why, and what they were planning to wear. Kerenza would be turning eighteen, as Katie just had, and they were both off to London this year for their first Season. Perhaps Mama would agree to let *her* stay home this year, since the family focus must be on Kerenza.

She would ask.

· · ·

"No," Mama said, looking up from her accounts in the morning room. "Absolutely not. Kerenza is merely there to become known and to acquire a little town bronze. She is *not* seeking a husband. *You,* on the other hand…" Mama regarded her with a dissatisfied frown. "You're good looking enough. You received—how many offers, in your first Season?"

"Seven." Seven men pawing at her hand and beseeching her with big eyes. She shuddered at the thought of marrying any one of them.

"And your second Season?"

"Four."

"And refused them all. Well, that was all right when you were younger, but it's time you chose a husband and settled down. You're twenty now. Females must marry, Melissa. It's the only way we gain any independence."

"But we do *not* gain independence, Mama. Instead of our father having power over us, our husbands have that power. We have no *rights!*"

"Lud, don't start that again. The world is as it is, and one must do the best one can within it."

That sounded logical, and yet it had a fallacy at the heart of it. "That presumes the world cannot change. But it can."

Mama tapped her quill on the ledger. "Perhaps it may. Not enough in our lifetime to make a difference, however. Deal with the world as it is, and choose a husband this Season. Or your father and I will choose one for you."

Cold settled in the pit of Melissa's stomach. Was this what panic felt like? The *idea* of marrying. Of being *touched* all the time. Of having no right to say *no*...that was terrifying. Her stomach roiled with nausea.

Mama looked back at the accounts, and sighed. She always had trouble with them.

"I'll do those, Mama," Melissa said. She could take refuge in the calmness of numbers. That would help. If she kept thinking about marriage, she would start to cry and rock and…other things which did not befit a lady.

"Oh, thank you!" Mama got up from the table. Melissa sat down, her water spaniel Argos at her side, as always. She picked up the quill and ran it down the first column of figures as Argos laid his head on her thigh, his warmth comforting. The world faded away as the numbers danced for her, bright and clean-edged. She sighed, and relaxed, and was only vaguely aware of her mother leaving.

She could rely on numbers. And on Argos.

CHAPTER 2

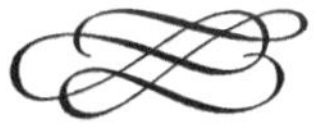

Charles watched as Melissa Trengrouse ran her pencil over the French dispatch. He could possibly have decoded it himself, if he'd had to, but it would have taken him twice as long and he likely wouldn't have been as accurate.

Castlereagh wouldn't thank him for returning with bad information. It was Wednesday. If Melissa could get this finished today, he would easily get to Dover by Friday.

They were in the small morning room rather than the library they normally worked in—pushed out by ball preparations, apparently. It was a cheerful yellow room with a nice aspect of the oak grove, but he ignored the view. Melissa was much better to look at.

She was so beautiful that gazing at her was like contemplating a great work of art. He wished that she affected him in other ways, but of course she didn't. Well, at least they were friends.

"No," Melissa said with her normal definite tone. "It's not a subscript. Look, if we invert it…you see? *Otakoustai.*"

"Ah yes." Charles nodded. "Far more likely."

Otakoustai was Ancient Greek for a scout or spy. Which would fit with what they knew about the French Provisional Government's approach to surrendering Paris—they would want to know everything they could about the occupying armies before they acceded to General Wellington's treaty demands. Although the armies had *entered* Paris, some on the French side were still plotting to expel them, and they would want to know the strength of those encamped outside the city.

When had the French started ciphering in Greek? A new author had clearly taken over the dispatches. From the upper classes. And they expected the receiver to be equally familiar with the language. Perhaps the rumours about Augustine being noble wasn't so far off the mark.

Someone cleared their throat and they both looked up, startled. Charles smoothly took the paper from the table and slid it into his pocket.

Demelza Mandeville stood in the doorway. Melissa's older sister, a recent widow, still pale in her blacks.

"That sounds interesting," she said.

"It is!" Melissa beamed up at her. "Charles always brings me the best puzzles." That caught at his heart. Decoding with Melissa was indeed the best kind of puzzle.

"Puzzles? Shouldn't you be helping Mama with the preparations for the ball?"

Oh, no. No, he could not allow this no

doubt very nice woman to misuse Melissa in such a way. Didn't this family realise what they *had*? One of the great minds of the nation, and she wanted it wasted on counting china and planning menus, like any ordinary debutante. Outrageous. He pushed down his anger and brought up his diplomatic smile.

Charles stood up, stretching the leg which still ached from his ride. Legacy of a musket ball he'd taken in the thigh in Spain. Melissa's spaniel, Argos, raised his head but then lowered it again as he realised Charles wasn't intending to go out the garden door. "A word with you, Lady Demelza?"

"When I was ten, you called me Demelza." She smiled to show she was joking.

"When we were that age, a lot was different." He led her into the passageway and checked quickly to make sure there was no one listening. Petroc knew the truth, and possibly her parents, but Demelza had been living in Gloucestershire for years and was uninformed.

"Demelza…I would appreciate it if you

allowed Melissa to keep working. She's translating a..an important document for me."

"From *Greek*? I didn't know you were an antiquarian."

He couldn't help smiling; his profession did require him to occasionally pretend to be an antiquarian, and he could be very convincing.

"From the Greek, yes. I suppose someone in this family should know apart from Petroc…Melissa has been helping me for some years with code breaking."

Demelza's mouth opened and closed, but she said nothing.

"I've been in His Majesty's service for quite a long time." His voice was mild, but he put a warning underneath. "But I would prefer that not be widely known."

She recovered her voice. "Why tell me, then?"

"Because this code is crucial to the safe re-establishment of France as a stable country. I can't tell you more, but Melissa is vital part of the effort to avoid another war. And she *cannot* be frittering her time away on ball preparations."

"I understand. I'll make sure she isn't disturbed." The woman looked oddly upset by the information, but that wasn't his problem.

His diplomatic smile again. "Thank you. I'm in your debt. I'll be gone by the end of the day." He bowed, just a trifle, and went back into the morning room.

"All well?" Melissa asked.

He nodded. "I've brought her into the secret of your work for me."

"Sensible. Otherwise she'd be a dog at my footsteps." Argos gave a quick bark at the word 'dog' and they both laughed.

As he sat, Melissa rose and closed the door, locking it. He nodded approval. Appalling behaviour, and scandalous if anyone realised they were locked in alone, but they really *couldn't* be interrupted again.

This message was too important to the continued safety of their troops.

· · ·

MAMA WOULD HAVE the vapours if she found out that Melissa had locked the door on herself and Charles. There was no other way. They simply *had* to finish this as quickly as possible.

Charles had his head down over the paper as she made her way back to the table, the gold flecks in his hair gleaming in the light from the windows. He looked up as she sat and they exchanged a smile of slightly guilty complicity.

He was like a Greek god—not one of the unpleasant ones, like Ares. Nor as arrogant and unjust as Apollo. More Hermes: clever, quick, funny with jokes she actually understood, prepared to lie in a good cause.

She approved of Charles. And his puzzles.

Several hours later she decided that this one, unfortunately, wasn't very interesting once decoded. Just a request for more information on the strength of the British forces, and their intentions with regard to the treaty, and directions to send a reply 'with all haste'. There was one tidbit: a promise of ten thousand francs if the agent could find out Castlereagh's full intentions regarding reprisals against France.

"Even with the currency affected by the war, that's a great deal of money," she observed as Charles folded up the papers and stowed them in his jacket's inside pocket.

"Too much. Unless the person is already well off, and requires an exorbitant bribe to make it worth his while. Or her while."

"Not her." Melissa ordered the blank sheets of paper on the desk, and rose to throw her working papers into the fire. "The grammatical forms were all masculine."

Charles smiled at her, that lovely smile which lit up his eyes. A smile he only gave when she'd been particularly clever. It was like an award.

"Of course they were. I should have seen that."

It was such a comfort, not having to hide her intelligence from Charles. Most men *hated* the idea that a woman might be cleverer than they. Not that Charles was *un*intelligent. On the contrary. He had a great brain for intrigue and understanding human motivation; it left her in awe, sometimes, how easily he controlled a conversation or soothed a feather she'd ruffled.

A shame he had to leave so soon.

"You can't stay for dinner?" she asked.

"Alas. I want to get a few miles in while the light is still good. I have to be in Dover by Friday morning."

She nodded. "I'll see you for Kerenza's ball?"

He bowed to her, but smiled. "I wouldn't miss it. Save me the supper dance."

As though they were mere acquaintances. A little mockingly, she curtsied, and he laughed as he left.

Charles always knew when she was joking.

ARRIVING ON THURSDAY EVENING, Charles didn't go all the way in to Dover. Castlereagh didn't like the noise and bustle of the central town, and always stayed at the recently re-built Marquis of Granby in Alkham, a few miles out of town.

He found his lordship in a private room, demolishing a sirloin of beef and a bottle of claret, along with Lt Vaughn, his aide-de-camp, seconded from the __th Foot. Vaughn greeted him and hastily stuffed a last mouthful of beef into his mouth, then picked up a dispatch case and went off.

"He's staying in England," Castlereagh said. "Commanding officer won't let him go when they're on home duties. Lot of farrago. Think next time I'll get a non-military fellow as an aide."

Was that a job for Charles? Hard to tell if that's what his lordship had meant. It wasn't a position he'd relish. Being at Castlereagh's beck and call all day, every day, wasn't appealing. He'd have to do it if asked, though. Perhaps that's what this meeting was really about. He could have sent the message with a trusted courier instead of bringing it himself.

The landlord set another place for Charles and brought up a capon and a mutton pie.

Castlereagh put out a hand and Charles placed the decoded document, plus the original, in it. His lordship read it quickly and harrumphed.

"Nothing there."

"No. But the original wasn't Russian. It was Ancient Greek."

Sharp bright eyes fixed on his face.

"A gentleman spy, eh? Damned disgrace."

"Indeed."

The capon was delicious. Charles kept eating while Castlereagh brooded. Then, abruptly, his lordship put the papers aside and took another bite, eating in silence. He put his fork down and leaned back in his chair, assessing Charles. It was only good manners to stop eating himself, but it was a deuced nuisance. He was starving.

"After the treaty...the Prime Minister isn't keen on keeping up the expense of a network of agents."

His stomach clenched. Since his job for the Crown wasn't official, his 'employment' could be ended at any time. He *needed* this job. Moreover, Britain needed information to secure its interests.

"That seems…short-sighted."

Castlereagh gave a bark of laughter. "You might put it so. But if that's going to happen, I want some of my men in key positions in the embassies. I'm thinking of you for Vienna."

Vienna. The centre of the Austrian empire. A seat of power.

"Metternich," Charles said. Klemens von Metternich was the Austrian chancellor, who had had an outsize influence on those treaties already drawn up between Europe and France during the Congress of Vienna. The treaty of Paris would be the last one.

Castlereagh slapped his thigh. "Exactly! Wily bird, and worth keeping an eye on. The congress put him in the driving seat, and he's not going to let go of the reins now. I want a man on the spot who understands the implications."

Well. That was quite a compliment.

"Vienna would be a good, central place from which to run a network of informers."

"An interesting idea. I'll think about that. But the position is yours if you want it."

He'd have to leave Melissa. Could he?

He scolded himself. They were just friends. That's all they could be. The two of them could, and would, correspond. Perhaps the family might even visit the Continent, now Bonaparte was defeated.

"I'm honoured, sir," he said, and Castlereagh nodded in satisfaction.

"You'll have some trumpery title. Attaché for trade, or something like that. But you'll be working for me, not the Ambassador."

There was a situation bound to cause problems. Still, his heart beat a little faster. A proper job, out in the open. It would be an adventure, even if leaving Melissa was the price he had to pay.

CHAPTER 3

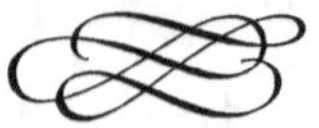

"Charles!" Melissa said. A knot in her chest loosened. There were *so many* people here for the ball; many she barely knew. The house was fuller than she'd ever seen it. Charles would be her refuge.

He smiled at her, that particular smile he gave no one else. 'Reporting for duty, sir!'

She beckoned him from the hall into the library as the servants took his luggage up to his usual room.

"I have bought a new translation of Oedipus the King, but I have a few quibbles with it," she said happily.

He rubbed his hands together in a parody of greed, and she laughed.

"Excellent!" he said. "Let us see this ridiculous attempt at translation."

Just an hour—even half an hour—with Charles would restore her equanimity and allow her to deal with the other guests. Thank God he came.

IT WAS DEUCED ODD, to be at Trengrouse Hall with no work to do. Normally, he arrived in a hurry, huddled with Melissa in the library, and then posted off to London as fast as he could with their results. Not for the first time, he wished she lived in London all year round, rather than just during the Season.

On his second day here, the day before Kerenza's birthday ball, he had no duties but to be an agreeable guest, so he enrolled Petroc in a games of billiards. One of the things Petroc could still do after losing his foot at Waterloo. Having been wounded himself in Spain, Charles understood the urge to get back to action, but it always set one back in recovery. Better for Petroc to have a quiet game of billiards than to be stumping all over the huge house on his crutches.

But they'd scarcely set the balls up when one of the footmen arrived with a message that the earl wanted to see him.

Odd. He'd never had a private conversation with Jory, Earl Trengrouse, before. A curl of worry unfurled in his gut. The earl knew, broadly speaking, about the work he and Melissa did. Had he inadvertently made trouble for Melissa? Taken up too much of her time?

Petroc grinned at him. "About time."

"Time for what?" Charles put his cue back in the rack and straightened his neckcloth.

"What do you think?"

Well, that was no help, and not at all reassuring.

He followed the footman to the earl's study.

Lord Trengrouse was standing by the window, but he came and sat behind his desk as Charles came in, and gestured to Charles to take the other chair.

Melissa resembled her father—not in looks, but in mannerisms. Neither of them liked parties, or loud noises, or fashionable chatter, and both were always followed by at least one dog.

The earl's spaniel lay happily on his special blanket, tussling with a bone. It was a homely sight, and Charles relaxed a little.

"So," the earl said brusquely, "when are you going to marry my daughter?"

He froze. What could he say? What *should* he say? Panic swamped him, which was ridiculous. He was a government agent, and had faced far more dangerous situations than this!

"You've been mooning over her for three years now. When she was younger, I admired your restraint in waiting until she was old enough—but she's twenty now, and almost on the shelf! She'll never accept anyone else while you're hanging around. Time to piss or get off the pot, man."

Charles swallowed hard. "I have been *working* with Melissa–"

"Oh, don't give me that nonsense about codes! She's a bright gel, but there are far cleverer fellows in London to do the government's business! It was a nice deceit, but it's gone far enough."

This grumpy old man was an idiot. Her whole family were idiots. Living here must be hell for her.

"Your daughter," Charles said, leaning forward for emphasis, "has one of the finest minds in England. Possibly in Europe. She has created the cipher we are currently using, and no one—not French, nor German, nor Russian—has been able to crack it. She has been a vital part of the war effort, and if you don't realise how extraordinary she is, you're a fool."

Trengrouse blinked at him, then smiled slowly. "You feel very strongly about this."

"I do."

"So, I repeat, when are you going to marry her?"

Damn.

Use an easy excuse.

"I'm not in a financial position to support a wife." Humiliating, but true. His father had gambled away most of Charles' inheritance.

Trengrouse waved that off. "Melissa's dowry will fix that. She's well endowed."

"I don't aim to be seen as a fortune-hunter."

"No such thing! You're an old friend of the family. Nothing could be more proper."

Time for the artillery to take the field.

"I will never marry. I am unable to give a woman children." There. *Take that and see how you like it.* Trengrouse started back a little, and cast a quick glance at his leg. Charles had visited here not long after he'd been wounded. Yes, let him assume that the wound had, well, castrated him. Mortifying, especially since it was untrue, but it would stop this nonsense in its tracks.

"I see..." The earl pulled at his lip, then

glared. "Then why the hell are you dangling around after Melissa?"

"I have *told* you–"

"Yes, yes, the war effort and so on. The war is over. Time for you to leave my daughter alone and let her find a husband who *can* give her children!"

Charles got to his feet, bowed, and went out.

What else could he do?

Was the earl right? If everyone had been assuming he and Melissa would marry, had other men not bothered to court her?

Had he doomed her to spinsterhood?

He would think himself a selfish, besotted fool, but the work was the work, and it was necessary. Even now the war was over.

The European powers were jockeying for position in the new map of Europe currently being negotiated in Paris. It would take months, and it was vital that they be able to convey messages secretly from London to the Paris embassy. Equally vital to know what messages the other powers were sending back and forth.

And at the centre of that was Melissa, who was twice the cipherer he was, and who had given them access to the new French cipher almost as soon as they started using it.

Damn her father and his conventional thinking. Melissa was an agent of the British crown, and should be treated as such.

His heart hurt at the thought her family might not allow him to see her in the future, or even correspond with her once he was in Vienna. She was the shining light at the centre of his life. What would he do without her?

Could he even leave her to go to Austria? He wasn't at all sure.

CHAPTER 4

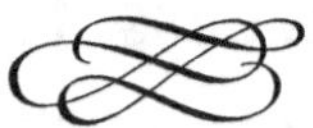

On the day of the ball, Melissa had no more excuses. There was nothing to code or decode, and Charles was spending all his time with Petroc. They had been friends at school and in the Army, until Charles had been wounded; no doubt they had a lot to catch up on.

So she dutifully went along to the ball-room and helped arrange flowers.

What this actually meant was that, by long tradition, she designed the flower arrangement, and everyone else copied it. This had the advantage that each arrangement was pleasingly symmetrical, and she wouldn't be irritated during the ball by catching sight of an untidy vase.

The flower arranging had brought in all the young ladies: Beatrice Marlowe and Katie Kelynack, as well as Demelza and Kerenza. Even Elestryn, her oldest brother Locryn's wife, had taken time out from running the household to help. Some of the men were there too: her brother Petroc and the younger Mr Muffet, son of a business acquaintance of her father's. He and Beatrice were both staying at Trengrouse Hall for the ball.

It was all going smoothly when Petroc hoisted himself onto his crutches and went over to Kerenza.

"Happy Birthday, Keri," he said, holding out a packet.

Kerenza put her hand out and looked surprised to be given papers instead of a present, but opened it eagerly, then looked up in astonishment.

"But-these are shares."

Women just weren't given shares. Ever. That was one of those stupid societal rules people were always trying to get Melissa to understand. Had she misunderstood this one?

"Yes," he said. "Held in trust for you. Mama and Lady Marlowe are your trustees. It should provide you with a little independent income."

Kerenza's eyes grew wide. She was very surprised. So Melissa *hadn't* misunderstood. This was an extraordinary thing for Petroc to do.

"Th-thank you." Kerenza showed the shares to Melissa and Beatrice at the arranging table.

"Why Kerenza?" Demelza asked. Melissa knew that tone; it meant someone was in trouble. It was a good question. Petroc had never given either Demelza or her shares.

He looked flustered; unlike the calm soldier he'd become when he went into the Army. Of course, losing his foot meant he wouldn't be a solider for long.

"I thought I'd talk to the others—Locryn and the others–" he said, "and see if we couldn't find parcels of shares for all of you. It's not good for a woman to be completely dependent on her husband. Or on getting a husband."

Shares for her too! That was good.

Beatrice stood up from her table, her cheeks pink. It wasn't worth trying to work out why. Melissa knew herself well enough to realise that she'd guess wrong.

"It certainly isn't," Elestryn said. "That was well thought of."

"You'll set a trend," Mr Muffet said. "I hope my sisters don't hear about this—it might bankrupt us!"

Petroc chuckled. "Do you have many?"

"Six!" Muffet said in tones of despair.

Everyone laughed. Melissa laughed too, gently. She was quite good at that: laughing when other people did, not too loud and not too long. Her mother had taught her how.

Elestryn joined her at the arranging table.

"It will be good for you to have money of

your own," she said. "That will mean that you won't *have* to marry, if you don't want to."

Melissa looked at her in shock. "Don't you think I should marry? Everyone else does."

Her sister-in-law scowled. "What *I* think doesn't matter. Not to anyone. But for *you*—I don't think you'd be happy in a normal marriage, Melissa. It's hard enough when you're both…both *committed* to it. If they forced you into a match…I think that would end badly, for you and for your husband."

Even she could see that Elestryn was probably talking about her and Locryn's marriage being difficult. Not a thing Melissa had ever thought about before. They'd been married when she was still in short skirts, and they had three children now. They were just *there,* a family within the larger Trengrouse family.

Elestryn had always seemed like a pattern-card of how a lady of quality should be. If *she* thought that perhaps Melissa shouldn't marry…but, oh! it would be so hard to withstand the pressure, the "talks", the "encouragement" she knew her parents were capable of. It would last for months, right up until she turned twenty-one and could decide who to marry—or *if* to marry—for herself.

For herself!

She drifted into a happy daydream of having a small house of her own. Somewhere nearby, so she could still sail with her twin, Ives.

As she finished the flowers and went up to change for the ball, she added details. Perhaps it could be the size of Semper Cottage, where Beatrice lived. Just big enough for her and a library and a couple of servants. With a guest room for Charles.

It would take a while for her to build her library, but she could borrow from Charles if she needed anything. He wouldn't mind.

He could come down from London with the dispatches and ciphers, and they could work amicably together in her very own library. Then they'd eat and sleep and get up the next morning to do it all again.

What a wonderful life!

"There," her maid Maryann said as she finished perfecting Melissa's hair. "You look like a princess! You'll have all the men buzzing after you like bees after a flower."

A shudder went through her at the thought. Such a contrast to her imaginings. Buzzing—that was *exactly* what it was like, being in company; as though a hive of bees was buzzing in her head.

Living alone and working with Charles would be so *calm*; so *interesting*. He could come often; more often than now, because he wouldn't have to need a reason. He'd just come whenever he chose.

Melissa rose and Maryann put her into her gown; a lovely dark green. She had been going to wear pale Pomona green but had decided yesterday that she did *not* want to be seen as a debutante on the Marriage Mart, so had chosen a gown in a deeper colour. Debutantes always wore pastels; her dress was one more suitable for a young matron. Her mother wouldn't be pleased, but perhaps this was a way of discouraging advances from men she couldn't imagine talking to for ten minutes, let alone marrying?

She sat as Maryann put Kerenza into her dress: white with blue ribbons. Her mind swerved back to the daydream.

A library, a study…no need for a breakfast room when it was just her. She could eat at her desk. How freeing! Charles wouldn't mind…

As though she turned a book the right way up and read it properly for the first time, she saw the pattern of life she'd daydreamed from a new angle.

It looked a lot like marriage.

Living with Charles would be *good*.

Could she…could she deal with all the other aspects of marriage, to have that companionship?

"Come on, Lissa!" Kerenza said impatiently. "It's time!"

Perhaps it was time. If she *could* deal with

those…intimate parts of marriage…she could have the independence and the happiness of intellectual equals living harmoniously together.

It was a price worth paying.

And it had the advantage that she wouldn't have to wait until she was twenty-one to do it.

THERE SHE WAS. Charles smiled up at Melissa as she came down the stairs. Green suited her. Seeing her always gave him joy; losing that privilege would hollow out his life. He shrugged away the thought. Sufficient unto the day…

As one of the peers present, he had to take the Dowager Countess Merryam in to dinner. Melissa was squired by a Mr Gunson, and had Ives, her twin, on her other side. Ives always sat next to Melissa; he was there, she'd told Charles, to guide her on the finer points of social intercourse. In other words, to tell her when someone was being sarcastic, or making a joke she didn't get.

They were a devoted pair. Ives was the only one of the family who really understood how brilliant Melissa was.

It was impossible to be sad or self-absorbed when sitting next to Phoebe, Countess Merryam. She was both charming and witty, and soon had him laughing. She was also uncomfortably perceptive.

"Melissa is still where she was a moment ago," she said dryly as the third course was brought in. "She won't run away during dinner. There's no need to keep glancing at her."

He blushed. "I'm sorry, Countess. I'm afraid I've been dashed rude."

"Much can be forgiven a pair of lovers." She patted his hand. "Honestly, though, Charles, why haven't you offered for the girl?"

Not her too! He stiffened up.

"I'm afraid there are reasons..."

She tapped him on the hand with her fan. "I suspect those reasons are wills-o-the-wisp, and would disappear with the clear light of day on them."

Was she right? No.

He couldn't offer any woman a true marriage. What he had to offer was unacceptable.

"WHAT ARE YOU GRINNING AT?" Melissa came up behind Ives and stood by his side as the musicians tuned up for the first dance.

"Nothing, Twin. Nothing you need be concerned about." Oh, dear. That was Ives' code for 'I'm going to get into trouble'.

"Another scrape? Just don't ruin Keri's party."

"Never fear." He grinned at her. She wished she could be more like him. He took everything so lightly.

"Mama says it's time for me to think about marriage," she said. "I don't think it's at all fair that she's not saying the same to you."

"Men get a few more years." Did Ives' tone mean he agreed with that? It was one of those things she was never sure of. But then he said it out loud. "It's not fair." That was Twin, always making sure she understood.

She nodded, satisfied. "If I have to marry, you should too."

"Heaven forfend!" He threw up a hand as though parrying a blow, and she laughed at what was clearly a joke. "I'm not the marrying kind, I don't think."

Why couldn't she have been born male? Life would be so much easier!

"I'm not either, but *I* don't get a choice," she said.

"If you truly were strongly against it, I don't think Mamma *or* Papa would force it." That wasn't what Mama had said, but perhaps she had misunderstood? No, she didn't think she had.

"They want me to have *children*!" She shuddered, and he grinned again, but it wasn't funny. Would *Charles* want to have children? It was a daunting prospect.

At least they would have nursemaids and nannies. Some of her siblings' friends had barely seen their parents while they were growing up, and they seemed to have survived well.

It wasn't the way *they'd* been brought up, but perhaps Charles had been raised in that fashion, and would think it perfectly all right.

She had raised puppies, after all. Could children be so much harder? Resolutely, she refused to think about pregnancy. If she wanted that enchanted life with Charles, she'd have to pay for it *somehow*. Traditionally, women paid with marital relations and children.

Surely she could manage what so many other women did?

CHAPTER 5

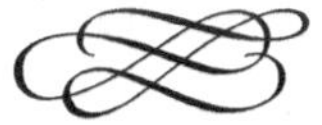

elissa had promised Charles a country dance and then the supper dance.

The country dance went by well enough, although Charles appeared to be somewhat distracted.

Her heart was beating faster than usual as he came to find her for the supper dance.

"Let's walk on the terrace instead," she said, tucking her hand into his arm.

Others were walking sedately on the terrace; it was well lit, and a couple of chaperones had taken up position at a small table, to prevent any indiscretions.

Privacy was easy enough to obtain without a scandal—they simply walked out of earshot, but stood where they were in full view of the chaperones.

"Melissa—"

She put up a hand. She had to say this now, and quickly, or she might lose her courage. She had a *chance*; to stop her mother's plans, to ensure her own happiness, to hopefully ensure Charles'.

"Charles. Mama wants me to marry. I have carefully considered who I might be prepared to live with, and yours was the only name on the list."

She waited. Was that clear enough? She could never tell these things.

"I think we should marry. Then we could continue our work uninterrupted."

His face looked…strange. As though conflicting emotions were crashing together in his mind. She had no idea what those emotions might be. Her stomach churned with nerves. Had she said something unforgive-able again? But this was *Charles*! He always understood her.

He tugged at his neckcloth.

"I-I *can't*. I'm sorry, Melissa, but I can't."

Oh.

There was a strange pain underneath her ribs. As though a knife slid past her lungs and into her heart.

Ridiculous. Yet there it was. She stood stock still, not knowing what to say, or what might make it all worse. The noise of the ball, the lights, the people, were suddenly *too much*. She needed Argos, and quiet, and the darkness...her breathing began to speed up.

Charles saw.

"I'm so sorry...Let's get you someplace quieter."

Her head was buzzing intolerably as they turned towards the ballroom. *Breathe. Breathe. You can control this. You're not a child any longer.* Bryok intercepted them before they'd gone more than a few paces.

"M'lord, there's a courier for you. Urgent."

That cut through the rising panic. A courier meant work.

Yes. Work would reduce all these *feelings* to their proper place. They went quickly through the supper room and into the main hall, where Johnson, a courier Charles often used, waited for them with a packet of papers in his hand. He looked exhausted, as though he had ridden hard to get there.

"Urgent, m'lord," he said to Charles.

Charles took it and gathered her with a glance.

"Bryok, get Johnson fed and find him a bed for the night," she said.

"Yes, miss."

There were card games going on in the library and other rooms had been commandeered for further ball-related activities. Only the morning room was exempt from the festivities. At least Argos was here, and came immediately to Melissa's side. She bent to hug him, as she did when she was upset.

Charles tamped down his emotions. It had wounded him to refuse Melissa. He'd wanted so badly to say, "Yes! Excellent idea!" but he couldn't cheat her so. She deserved a better man than he.

They sat side by side at the table and looked at the papers.

"I think it's coded in the *Grande Chiffre*," Melissa said. That was the cipher Napoleon had used. The Russians had found the code book which allowed them to decipher it in an abandoned baggage train outside Moscow. The Russians hadn't broadcast that they'd broken the code, and Britain certainly hadn't either. The French might have suspicions about their great cipher being broken, but they had no proof, so it wasn't unlikely that some diplomats were still using it.

"Let's get to it, then," he said.

Silently, they worked through the dispatch, both of them making copies and working through it line by line. Most of it was already known to them: the French desire to maintain their Italian lands, for example. The second page was more interesting. An assignation between the new French ambassador and a French agent, Augustine, in London, in two nights' time.

They'd been trying to find out who Augustine was for some months. It had to be an English government operative. Someone who had access to classified information, and had been betraying to the French all of Britain's intentions regarding the Paris Treaty terms, making it almost impossible to negotiate. Without a treaty, Europe would be plunged back into war. Charles shuddered at the thought.

Stopping Augustine could save the peace effort. He had to get to London before that assignation, and take a cadre of troops to arrest Augustine.

"I have to take this to London immediately." He parcelled up his copy of the decoded message, together with the original. Melissa looked up at him with perfect faith.

Was that a shadow behind her gaze? He felt like a cad, leaving her so soon and without a proper conversation. *Needs must when the devil drives.*

"I'll be back as soon as I can," he said. She nodded. She'd barely said a word to him the whole time, just worked silently as the noise of the ball faded away, the carriages had trundled down the drive, and the house had retired to bed.

"It will be all right, Melissa." It had to be. He couldn't bear it if he'd hurt her irreparably.

"It will *not* be all right if I am forced to marry someone else." Her voice was matter-of-fact, yet it still hit him with the force of a blow.

"Don't do that unless you really want to."

Sensing her distress, Argos laid his head on her lap and she stroked his ears. Thank God for Argos. She looked so fragile.

"You'd better go, Charles."

She didn't look at him as he left to change into riding gear. If he changed horses frequently, he could make it to London in twelve or thirteen hours.

He couldn't let himself dwell on the idea of marrying her. He focused on the road, thanking God for the westering full moon, and urged his gelding to go faster.

SLOWLY, Melissa gathered her copies of the dispatch together and went to the library to lock them in her desk.

Now that the work was over, the pain came back. She sat at the desk and tried to breathe, rocking back and forth, Argos's head in her lap.

She had misunderstood, again. All this time. All this time she had thought Charles was at least her friend. But the look on his face—the *panic*—when she had suggested marriage…would a friend look like that?

How could she have misunderstood him so completely? What had she missed? Had it always just been about his work? Was the only value she had for him as a cipherer?

Shame swept over her. She was so *stupid*! She had taken his normal friendliness as something more. Something warmer. Getting it all wrong, as she always did when people's feelings were involved.

Over and over, she went through each moment they'd spent together, looking for the clues she had missed. If she could figure it out, at least she'd know what not to do next time she saw him.

If she ever saw him again.

Her dream of a happy household, dedicated to research and ciphering, evaporated. An illusion she had created to comfort herself.

She should have known that no one who really *knew* her would want to live with her. She was too...odd. She'd always been odd. Had never been like the others. Didn't understand jokes, said the wrong thing, was overwhelmed so easily...the buzzing rose in her head and her heart beat faster and faster...Argos nudged her hand, and she slid down to the floor so he could climb into her lap, like when she was little and had run to the kennels whenever she felt it was all *too much*. That she was going to fragment and float off into the sky in pieces. There, she would sit and rock and the puppies would climb on her and she would hug them and smell their deep, complex scent, and feel the weight of them all on her and that would pull her back to the earth.

That child had wondered if perhaps she was a changeling, and the real, human, Melissa Trengrouse was off in Fairyland.

Nothing so simple.

If Charles couldn't bear the thought of marrying her—Charles, who really knew her —it was clearly impossible that any other man would bear with her...her idiosyncrasies. She would have to live alone.

She rocked and petted Argos, and tried to conjure up the image of the life she'd been so happy to imagine only last night. That cottage, with its library...it seemed so cold and empty when she couldn't imagine Charles into it.

She would live and die alone.

Argos's fur felt odd. She looked down and realised it was wet. She'd been crying, and hadn't noticed.

That was bad. She had to be *careful*. To pay attention. To monitor herself at all times, and make sure that she wasn't causing anyone distress. It would hurt the family to see her crying.

Only Ives would take it in stride, as he did everything about her. *He* loved her as she was.

Hope sparked in her chest. Once they turned twenty-one, they could move to Ives' estate in Norfolk, Kirwich Manor, and live together there. She had never thought she would do that, because she didn't want to be a burden on Ives, but if she had her own shares, as Petroc said, she could support herself.

It wouldn't be *good*, as it might have been with Charles. It would be bearable, however, and perhaps she could continue to do the government work.

They would probably assign her a new colleague; Charles wouldn't want to come back and face her after this. Even she knew that would be uncomfortable.

She had ruined everything. A wail rose up in her chest but she bit it down and buried her head in Argos's neck, rocking them both. He turned his head to lick her salty cheek and snuggled in.

With Argos, she could get through tonight. She was an *adult*, and she would survive this feeling of breaking apart and lying in pieces. She would put herself back together before morning.

Then no one would know how supremely foolish she'd been, to think that a man like Charles could possibly choose someone like her.

CHAPTER 6

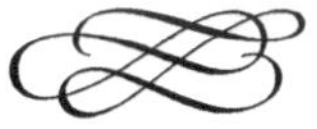

Charles grabbed some breakfast while his horse was being changed at an inn in Yeovil. Ham and eggs, some small ale. He could barely force it down. Every time he took a breath, he had to push away the image of Melissa's face after he'd rebuffed her, shocked and hurt.

On the ride, he'd had time to realise how badly he'd behaved.

"I can't." What kind of response was that to a woman—a *beloved* woman—who had suggested marriage? Bad enough to refuse her. *Shocking* to refuse her! To do it in such a bald and insulting way was unforgiveable.

He'd been lucky she'd agreed to work with him on this message.

Most women wouldn't have spoken to him again.

Melissa was extraordinary. If only…

It was no use yearning after what might be when you knew it *couldn't* be. She deserved a whole man, a full, proper man.

He just hoped it would be someone who understood her as he did.

MELISSA MANAGED to get back to the bedroom she was sharing with Kerenza for the duration of the ball house party. She crept in as the sky began to lighten, but that was a summer dawn, hours before she'd be expected to be awake.

For a moment, she stopped, nonplussed. How would she get out of her dress and stays without Maryann to help?

Shrugging, she lay down on the bed in

her ballgown, and stared at the ceiling, pushing away thoughts of Charles, silently reciting *The Iliad* in Ancient Greek for at least an hour before she slept.

WHEN SHE CAME into the hall after nuncheon, there was a great kerfuffle going on.

"Wish me happy, Twin," Ives said to her. Oddly, he had his hand on Katie Kelynack's waist. "We're married. Eloped."

Ives was married.

Married. Melissa breathed deeply. It gave her a kind of panic, to think that he had somehow left her behind. They had always been in step, but now... Her own marriage seemed suddenly inevitable, but who would she marry if Charles didn't want her?

And *why*? Why had he and Katie done it?

"Kitty's mamma doesn't approve of me as her husband. Too harum scarum and no title." Ives tucked Katie's hand under his arm.

"So we ran away to Truro and m'godfather married us by special licence!"

Nonsense. They weren't in love. She would have known if Ives were in love. He had planned a prank last night at the ball. It had gone wrong, and he'd had to marry Katie. That was the only explanation. Clearly elopement was the story they were telling, so she should support Twin in the only way she could.

"That was very silly of her," she said calmly. "You will make an excellent husband, Twin."

He smiled gratefully at her.

Her vision of a life with Ives at Kirwich Manor vanished like mist when the sun hit. A foolish fancy. Ives was properly human. He was always going to end up married, and what wife would want an odd, unpopular sister living with her?

She panicked internally. *Don't show it. Be a lady.*

Unobtrusively, she backed away and made it safely to the library. She had to open the door again when Argos scratched at it; she had left him behind but, good boy that he was, he had found her.

She had to find something to *do*.

Blindly, she went by habit to her desk and got the papers from last night out of the locked drawer, using the key she kept always in her petticoat pocket.

There had been something about that dispatch. Something not quite right. They had done a quick, rough job of decoding it, but…

There was a loud crashing going on in the china room. Really, couldn't people leave her alone to work! A few minutes later, a man walked out to a carriage which had drawn up, holding some kind of ape. A baboon? How odd.

The animal looked over the man's shoulder and saw her through the window. It grinned, cheekily. Kerenza followed it, patting its hand. She was dealing with it all, then. Good.

The baboon's cheeky grin stayed with her, but she shrugged it away.

She examined her copy of the message again, and realised that Charles had mistakenly left her the original. Even better, and he had a good copy—when she made a copy, she copied *everything*. Words, blots, scribbles, watermarks: everything. She had traced the watermark minutely. It had been unusual…

She took it to the window to see it in better light. The morning sun picked up the surface irregularities. There, the watermark wasn't *exactly* as she'd copied it.

It wasn't a watermark at all, it was an impression, pushed into the paper *after* manufacturing.

She had thought it was a fleur-de-lis, a popular French mark denoting high quality paper. But it was feathers. Three feathers, with a banner underneath. The banner wasn't clear enough to show words, but she knew what was written there nonetheless: ICH DIEN.

The badge of the Regent, the Prince of Wales.

This letter had *not* come from France, but from here in England. From Augustine, who apparently had access to the Regent's stationery.

The coding had been in the *Grande Chiffre.*

If Augustine was one of Prinny's inner circle, he would certainly know that the English had the key to that cipher. The message had been meant to be decoded.

A deep chill went through her.

It was a decoy. The assignation, the content of the message, all fake, designed to draw out His Majesty's agents and put them on the wrong track. Keep them busy with something nonsensical while the real spies performed some other task.

She must get a message to Charles *immediately.* His courier—Johnson. Johnson could take the message. His own horse would be exhausted after yesterday's hard ride. He could use Ives' second horse; Peony was rested and in good form. Twin wouldn't mind. She'd have given Johnson her mare, but it was trained only to sidesaddle.

Money. He would need money. She kept some pin money in her library drawer. Was it enough? It would have to be.

She ran to the stables and ordered a groom to saddle Peony. Johnson was sitting at Bill Coachman's table in the tack room. Breathless, she explained.

Johnson leapt to his feet and made for the horse.

"Here are funds," she said, pushing her purse into his hands. "I don't know if you'll need more—if it's not enough, tell them to bill Trengrouse Hall. Tell him: the message is fake. A decoy."

Johnson nodded grimly. He still looked tired, but he sprang onto Peony easily enough.

"Don't tarry," she said.

He pulled his forelock and set off at a canter, straight across the south lawn towards the toll road. Good man. She would deal with her father's annoyance about the lawn later.

Foolishly, she still had the original dispatch clutched in her hand.

Just as well. This was crucial evidence, and should be entrusted only to Charles. Besides, there was something there that had been very strange…

Back in the library, she pored over the watermark/impression. She was fairly sure that the Prince of Wales symbol had five jewels shown on the band under the feathers. Debrett's would show it.

Yes, the picture in Debrett's was quite clear. Five jewels.

On this, the two jewels on the sides had been rubbed out, perhaps with the blunt end of a pencil. There were only three.

That had to mean *something*.

She sat, reading over the original message and the decoded version.

Three jewels.

Three.

What if the decoded message hid another layer? A third message.

In a different cipher.

Horrified, she examined it again. It was certainly possible. It would explain some oddities in the language of the message.

But which cipher? The vista of a lovely day of deciphering spread out before her. *That* would calm her down properly.

No, she didn't have time to decipher it now.

For a moment, she was caught: she had to get news of the underlying message to Charles, but Johnson was gone, so she'd have to organise some other way of getting Charles the news—and she *also* had to decode that deeper message. She couldn't do both. If she waited to send the message until after she'd done the decoding, it might be too late. *Would* be too late.

Panic hit her, but she crouched down so Argos came and snuffled at her neck. She hugged him and breathed.

Of course.

She *could* do both, if she went to London herself and decoded the message along the way.

Running up to her room, she asked Maryann to put up a valise with a few days clothes in it, changed hastily into a carriage outfit, and ran back down to find Ives.

He was in the drawing room with the others, but came out to her at a tip of her head. She explained the situation, the original message still clutched in her hand. He cast a panicked look back into the drawing room. At Katie. His new wife.

"I can't go with you, Twin. Any other time…but it would be wrong to desert Katie today."

A flare of annoyance gave way to pity. Ives hadn't asked for this marriage, and he was right. He couldn't leave Katie alone to face up to the consequences of *his* prank.

"Lion is leaving this morning," he said. "He's giving Felix a lift back to London."

"Perfect." A little pressure lifted from her.

Maryann arrived with her valise and what seemed like a worried face. "Take that out to the stable and get it put on Mr Endellion's coach."

"Yes, miss."

As if called, Endellion came down the stairs carrying his greatcoat.

"I need to go to London with you, Lion," Melissa said. "I'll just get my writing kit."

"Do I want to know why?" Lion was trying to be funny, but his eyes were sombre.

"I'll tell you in the coach." He nodded, and Melissa ran to the library to catch up pencils, paper and ruler. As she arrived back in the hall, the whole family seemed to have boiled out of the great room, her parents in the forefront.

"What's this?" her father demanded. "You can't go to London on a whim, Melissa. Who'll chaperone you? Wait a few weeks and–"

"I can't wait. Charles may be in danger." She kept her voice level, as she always did. If she shrieked and screamed, they just locked her up in her room. She had to be calm, but it was so hard, with worry about Charles building up behind her breastbone.

"Ridiculous," her mother said. "This cloak and dagger nonsense with Charles has to stop, Melissa. He's just amusing himself with you–"

She spoke between her teeth, in a tone she'd never used in her life before.

"I am going to London." She stared each parent in the eyes. "Charles' life may be in danger. At the very *least*, he is going into a dangerous situation without all the facts. I can get him those facts, but only if I leave *now*."

"You're overestimating your importance–" her mother started.

"No, Mama." Astonishingly, it was Demelza who stepped forward. "Charles himself told me how crucial Melissa's work is to the safety of this country. We have to help her."

"But she can't go unchaperoned!" her mother almost wailed.

"She's not. She'll be with two of her brothers," Felix said. He was the quiet one of the family, usually off at the mines, and rarely intervened in his siblings' lives.

"I'm not letting her go haring off–" her father began, and her mother and the others began to talk over each other until the buzzing got louder and louder in Melissa's head.

"Be QUIET!" she shouted.

Astonished, they stared at her in silence. "I am going. I don't care if I'm ruined, or whatever you're so worried about. Charles is in danger and I *will* stop that." She breathed hard, but got hold of herself. "Endellion, can we go *now*?"

"Absolutely." Endellion had his 'Lion' face on, the one that said he didn't care what the family thought. He put a hand under her elbow and ushered her out to where his carriage was waiting, with her valise safely stowed on top. Argos at her heels, she got in, followed by Lion and Felix, and the steps were put up.

The wheels crunched against the gravel as the horses took up the strain and set off.

To London.

CHAPTER 7

With Castlereagh out of town, Charles needed his aide-de-camp, Lt Vaughn. Vaughn could organise the troopers they would need to take this nest of spies. Six or eight should do it; enough to surround a house.

Unfortunately, Vaughn was in barracks in Windsor, Boniface told him with a kind of sour pleasure. Damn. He'd practically ridden right past there.

"He *said* he was responding to orders, but if I know young officers he'll be taking a holiday, getting drunk in the mess and playing cards all day."

Who else? He and Petroc had been in the 10th, the Prince of Wales' Hussars, but they were in the Army of Occupation in Paris.

"May I ask the problem, my lord?" Boniface asked.

"I need troopers."

The clerk's eyes lit up. "I can help with that. We have troopers guarding the entrances. It will do them good to get off their lazy bottoms and do some real work."

Charles wanted to smack himself. Of course there were troopers. The Life Guards had the duty at the moment, and they had a command centre in the basement.

"Thank you, Mr Boniface."

He hastened down the stairs and was relieved to find Luke Forester in charge of the guard. They knew each other from Corunna, where both Charles and the then-lieutenant had been injured. Forester recovered enough to stay in the Army; Charles hadn't, although his health had improved substantially since then. He could even run, now, although not far.

"I see you've come up in the world!" Charles said.

Luke grinned. "Yes, it's Captain now, and I'll have a bit of respect from a civilian, thank you."

"Yessir Captain sir! Seriously, Luke, I need a favour, and you need to keep it under your hat until at least tomorrow."

"Ohoh! An intrigue! Who's the lady in question?"

This was one thing he didn't miss about the Army; the constant, never-ending joking about women and sex. He'd had a reputation as being strait-laced, which had just made him a target as a subaltern for the hearty bullies. Promotion over them all had saved him.

"No such thing. This is business."

Luke waved Charles to the battered visitors' chair and sat behind an equally battered desk. At least the room had a fire; that was its only comfort.

"I see they're showering you with the luxuries due to a returned soldier."

Making a face, Luke shrugged. "At least we have something to do, even if it is standing around and watching clerks go in and out with paper. I'd rather be here than back in the barracks, polishing medals, or at home, being condescended to by m'brother's wife."

Luke was a younger son, and lived off his wages, as Charles had when he was in the Hussars. His family had bought him his commission and felt they'd done all they needed to. There were a lot of younger sons like that; although fewer, he thought sadly, since Waterloo.

Time to get to business.

"Captain, I need at least six and preferably eight troopers to apprehend and arrest a nest of spies tonight."

"So *that's* what you've been doing for the Foreign Secretary! I *knew* you hadn't turned into a clerk!" Luke grinned. "What you need, my lad, is eight troopers and their captain. There's no chance I'm missing out on this."

MELISSA PORED over the hidden message, ignoring the bumps and jolts of the road.

Not *Le Grande Chiffre*; something else. Something new.

She wrote out the first few words of the decoded layer of the message, and then tried half a dozen ciphers on them.

Nothing. Somehow, the memory of the baboon's cheeky grin bobbed up in her memory.

It was bare-faced cheek to use the Prince Regent's own stationery in order to trap a Crown agent.

It would be bare-faced cheek to use the Crown's own new cipher to send a message to his associates.

A cipher which Melissa had invented.

Yes! It was a matter of moments to prove it. How *dare* he!

As she swiftly decoded the message, she paled.

The message wasn't a decoy: it was a trap. The third layer was quite clear. Charles would go to the supposed assignation. He was to be kidnapped along the way and taken prisoner.

The last part of the message, with the address and details of where he was to be held, was double-coded, she thought. Grimly, she set to work.

An hour later, Felix patted her leg. "Time to stop and eat, Melissa."

They were in a coaching inn. She hadn't noticed when they stopped. She wanted to scream and cry that they *couldn't* stop, they had to hurry; but the horses needed to be changed, so they had time—just—to eat.

It was rational to do so; to eat and drink and keep her strength up.

She didn't have to like it.

Felix helped her down from the coach and Argos sprang after her, eager to explore. Endellion had already gone inside to order their meals. It was dark. She had no idea how long they'd been travelling. There had been one stop before this, she vaguely remembered, but Lion had brought food back to the coach that time.

"How far from London are we?"

"We'll be there by mid-afternoon," Felix said. He was a mathematician, an engineer. She could trust his estimates.

Good. Good. They should be there in time.

Inside the inn, she ate the cold beef and the hot soup without thought, but made sure to give some to Argos, under the table.

"Melissa," Endellion said. "Just how important *is* this? Charles Goddard works for the Foreign Secretary at times, I'm told by my—er, my business associates."

Endellion was an importer and exporter. He had worked with Charles, she knew, to get messages smuggled into Spain via Africa.

"So do I." She pushed her plate away, suddenly nauseated. "I'm one of their chief cipherers, although they don't know that."

Felix didn't look surprised. "Better that way," he said. "Castlereagh wouldn't trust anything done by a woman."

She hesitated. "I'll tell you all about it in the coach. I may need your help."

Nodding, Endellion pushed some bread and butter towards her. "Eat," he said. "We'll need our strength."

She ate, although it almost choked her, while Felix took Argos out for a short walk. She had to keep up her strength. For Charles.

CHAPTER 8

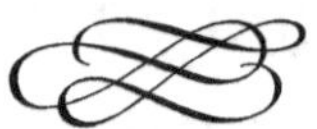

Charles headed home to bath and change.

He'd get the troopers there well before the assigned time, and place them inconspicuously. It was a warehouse in Shadwell, the message said. There should be alleys enough to hide in; and if not, they'd commandeer someone's store or front parlour.

An ugly part of town, Shadwell, close to the docks on the Thames, but a good place to meet if you didn't want to be seen by Society. It was a poor area; always poor and intermittently well off, depending on what ships were in and how much stevedoring there had been that day.

They'd get no help from the inhabitants, that was certain. More likely to be pelted with bottles and rotten vegetables.

You couldn't blame them. There was far too much poverty in the slums, and the living conditions were atrocious. He'd sponsored bills in the House of Lords to try to force slum landlords to maintain their properties, but too many peers were landlords themselves, and cared nothing for the poor.

He lived in rooms in Albany; he's spent pretty much everything he had on the set, as apartments in Albany were called, but it had been worth it. With lodging secured, his salary from the Crown covered his needs and his man's pay. Just. He'd live in the embassy in Vienna, no doubt, so he'd be able to rent the rooms out while he was gone.

Hopefully, that would be enough to cover the much-better clothing he'd need to buy if he was going to masquerade as an attaché.

Striding past the Burlington Arcade, he

was hailed by Joshua Leigh. A Member of Parliament, but from a wealthy family, Leigh was a crony of the Prince Regent's, which was odd for a man only in his early thirties. He and Charles had been allies in a couple of bills; he putting them forward in the Lower House, Charles in the Lords.

"Leigh," Charles acknowledged. "Sorry, in a bit of a rush."

"You're looking a bit worse for wear, old fellow." Leigh raised a supercilious eyebrow; Charles supposed he did look rough, having ridden through the night and no time to freshen up.

"Needs must when the devil drives, I'm afraid."

Leigh's mouth quirked up. "I'm sure it does. I'll let you get on then. But next week we really must discuss the Catholic Emancipation Bill." Casually, he leaned against the entrance to the Arcade. A long, lean man, with dark hair and equally dark eyes, he attracted admiring looks from the ladies passing by.

"You know I'm behind you on that, but we'll have trouble getting the numbers."

"Even so." Leigh nodded and straightened. He was with a man Charles only knew by sight. Hilary, Baron Ellis. Another of Prinny's friends, but older, a short, stocky, olive-skinned fellow, who scowled at Charles and slapped Leigh on the back.

"Yes, yes." Leigh tipped his hat to Charles in a cursory acknowledgement of his rank, and they went on.

He only made it a few steps when Lt Stewart, of the Scots Greys, bumped into him and he was forced into another conversation. He *couldn't* look as though he had urgent business; he was supposed to be a man of leisure, apart from attending Parliament.

"Did you know Mrs MacDonald has gone back to Northumberland?" Stewart asked. "To live with her brother."

Mrs MacDonald was the widow of a captain in Stewart's regiment, who'd been Charles' friend in Spain. Lachie MacDonald had died at Waterloo. He couldn't rush out of this conversation without looking like an unfeeling cad. He had time, surely, for a few words?

"No doubt best for her," he said.

Ten minutes later, Stewart moved on, with an invitation for him to come to the Horse Guards for mess night soon.

Finally. Next time he bought a set of rooms, he'd choose somewhere out of the way, like Argyll Street, where no one knew him.

His man, Barker, was waiting for him, worry stamped on his face. He'd sent a message from the stables when he'd first arrived, to let Barker know he was back in Town.

"A quick change and I'll be off," Charles told him. Barker's mouth firmed in disapproval. "Don't be like that, man, it's the king's business."

"I respectfully suggest eating first, my lord. I have placed a small repast in the dining room. And I have drawn a bath."

They were both good ideas. No telling when he'd next be able to eat. An old campaigner, Charles knew that food and rest were the key to success in almost anything, and he'd had none for too long.

"Coffee would be useful. A quick bath, and then I'll eat. I'd rather wash the road off me first."

Barker looked him up and down with a slightly exaggerated disdain. "Indeed."

Grinning, Charles tapped him on the upper arm as he went past to the bedroom. Barker loved to put on the act of the upper class valet, but he'd been a private with a thick East End accent when Charles had chosen him as his batman.

How they'd both changed since then.

Inevitably, his thoughts went to Melissa. Had he hurt her beyond reconciliation? He had to explain to her, had to soothe whatever insult he'd given her.

After tonight.

Tomorrow, he'd ride back to Cornwall and apologise.

Profusely.

· · ·

AN HOUR LATER, as the sun was beginning to decline into the long summer evening, he left Albany and hailed a hackney to take him to meet Forester and his squad at Whitehall. He should still be able to get there before the time Luke said they'd set out. If he missed them, he'd go on to the location they'd chosen as a base for the raid.

As he settled into his seat and tapped on the roof to let the driver know he could loose the horses, a burly man climbed in the other side.

"Taken, I'm afraid," Charles said. He caught the look on the other's face and brought his hands up, but the door on his side opened and something hit him on the head. He pitched forwards, thinking, *Stupid, stupid!*, then he went under.

THEY WENT STRAIGHT TO CHARLES' house.

"You stay in the carriage," Felix told Melissa. "You can't be seen to enter Albany.

Besides, no women allowed. I know where his set is. I'll bring him out."

Melissa waited impatiently. Felix was right, of course. The doorman would never let her in, and it would ruin her to be seen here, a place where only bachelors lived.

The wait was agonising. Only a few minutes later, though, Felix ran down the steps and hastened towards them.

"He's gone already. To Whitehall, his man says."

"He's gone to get support. Sound decision," Endellion said. Felix gave the coachman the direction and they set off. At least it was Endellion's driver, used to the streets of London. He knew where he was going, and would get there the quickest way.

Melissa forced herself to breath deeply. They had to arrive in time.

That was illogical. She *wanted* them to arrive in time, but there was no guarantee.

At Whitehall, she had to stay in the coach again, but this time it was Endellion who went in. "I know a fellow in the Foreign Office," he said reassuringly. "He'll trust me enough to help me find Charles. And find out if Johnson made it in time."

That was true. If Johnson had reached him, Charles would know it was a decoy, and not go. She was worrying for nothing.

Felix patted her hand. "It'll be all right, Lissa. We'll find him. Never fear."

Her brothers were good men. But they weren't realists.

Her fears lodged hard under her heart when Endellion came back ten minutes later, accompanied by a man in a Light Guards uniform. A trooper.

They both got in.

"My lady," he said. "Private Shepherd, at your service. Lord Westholm hasn't been here, and Johnson only came five minutes ago. Lame horse, and he wouldn't give anyone else the message. We've sent a rider to the captain already. He's just set out. But… earlier, the captain received a note from his lordship, saying he would meet us at the rendezvous point."

His face was grave.

"Barker said he left Albany *for Whitehall* more than an hour before we got there. He should have been here with time to spare before they set out," Felix said. His face, always so easy to read, was full of worry.

A cold calm descended on her. "They have him."

"I'm afraid so," Private Shepherd said.

"Then it's just as well I know where they've taken him."

The private brightened. "Excellent! If you give me the address, I'll go to the captain and bring the squad there straight away."

Melissa gave him the address, a house in Hammersmith. The opposite direction from Shadwell, where the troopers would be waiting for Charles. Private Shepherd ran back, heading around the side of the building, no doubt to the stables.

"It'll take too long for him to get to Shadwell and then get the troopers back to Hammersmith. If they've abducted Charles, it's to get information. They'll–" She caught her breath, and then went on resolutely. "–they'll torture him. We have to go now. They can't have too many men. Not in the middle of London."

She stared both of her brothers down. Felix threw up his hands.

"Yes. All right."

Endellion nodded. "Hammersmith, you say? I have a warehouse there. I think I know that address." Felix looked worried again. "Should we call the watch?"

"No," Melissa said.

"King's business," Endellion said. "Charles wouldn't thank us for broadcasting his dealings all over London." He put his head out the window and gave his coachman the address. "Sorry, Jim," he added. "Last stop before home."

"Right you are, sir," Jim's voice came back, sounding tired. He and his offsider had been swapping driving duties all through the long trip.

Endellion opened up one of the squabs behind his head and pulled out a box.

As they made their ways through increasingly crowded streets, he opened the box. Pistols. She remembered. He'd bought them when he came home from India, a present to himself for his success there. Lion was a crack shot. All her brothers were, trained since birth to hunt. And fight. He handed one to Felix and they set about loading them.

The smell of gunpowder was comforting. They weren't going in unarmed. And no one would expect them, because no one knew she could decipher the third layer of the message. Also comforting.

What were they doing to Charles, while this carriage made its excruciatingly slow passage through the London streets as the twilight faded? For once the noise and the sense of being surrounded by far too many people didn't distress her.

She had greater troubles to bear than that.

CHAPTER 9

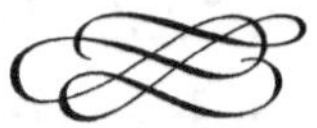

"Look out! He'll shoot the cat when he comes to."

The voice was right. He felt damnably sick.

A basin was presented and he cast up his accounts into it.

A moment later he collected himself and looked around. His head was splitting, but he could see well enough.

A largish room, perhaps an artist's studio? There were shelves at the back and sides. Could have been an empty library. The floors were smooth, and the walls well plastered. The windows were shuttered, but some light filtered through. He could see the two men from the hackney, both large. Much larger than he. One dark, one fair. They observed him with satisfied grins.

He was tied to a chair, the ropes cutting into his wrists. Tied well, too—these were skilled hectors, then, accustomed to keeping prisoners. For ransom? No. This was the king's business.

"Do you know who you're working for?" he managed out of a dry mouth. "The king's enemies."

They both laughed.

"We work for whoever pays us, mate," the one with fair hair said. "Been a long bloody time since I took the king's shilling."

His companion laughed. "And I never did, so the king never paid me a penny. Took coin, more like, like all the gentry."

As one, they both spat on the floor.

"So you're happy to be traitors?"

Casually, the dark-haired one back-handed him across the cheek. Dazed, he shook his head.

"Keep y'r trap shut, matey."

That was odd. They weren't planning on making him talk?

"Oh, go on," the other said. "Let him gabble. The more he talks, the oftener we can hit him. Augustine *said* to keep him quiet."

This struck them both as funny and they doubled over laughing.

"I fancy a drink," Fair Hair said, wiping his eyes.

"Off you go to the Black Lion, then. Some Mother's Ruin would hit the spot, and mind you get a good jug of ale to go with it."

So Dark Hair was the boss. Fair Hair went out, and the other sat at a small table with two chairs, the only other furniture in the room, and lit a lantern. It was almost dark.

They had taken him on his way to the rendezvous, and he couldn't believe that was a coincidence.

If they knew the British had broken the

cipher, Luke Forester was on a wild goose chase. They would have taken him in the opposite direction to Shadwell. Fools not to.

Which meant no one was looking for him.

Who was Augustine? The traitor had to be someone within the Foreign Office.

Boniface knew he'd deciphered the message.

Hard to believe it was him. He'd been Castlereagh's loyal attack hound for years.

Luke? Impossible.

But living off an officer's pay—even a captain's—wasn't easy, especially for those who'd been raised in comfort, such as he and Luke. A big enough bribe…

He didn't want to believe it was Luke. And Vaughan, whom he'd prefer by far to be the traitor, wasn't on site when he came in with his request for troopers.

Could he have been informed by Boniface, quite innocently?

How he hated having to suspect people he knew and liked! An instinctive shake of his head made him feel every bruise. His lip was bleeding, and the side of his face was on fire. Not the time to think about that.

Dark Hair pulled out a small clay pipe and a penknife and began carve a small piece of tobacco from a block in a tin. He was concentrating on shaving the tobacco thinly so it would burn easily.

Now.

Old habits died hard, and he'd never got over the habit of leaving a knife in his boot; useful in Spain, when one could be in digs without any crockery or cutlery, and even more useful in the long days in hospital, recovering from his wound, when he had whittled pipes to share with his fellow convalescents, like Luke.

They hadn't tied his ankles. By stretching down, and pressing his legs as far back as he could…

There.

He shuffled the small knife up higher into his hand, and angled it to start cutting.

· · ·

HAMMERSMITH WASN'T A SLUM AREA, not like the docklands, despite being near the Thames, but it wasn't affluent, either. There were closed shops and the houses needed paint.

The Black Lyon inn, however, was doing good business, with a crowd of both women and men milling outside, drinking from pewter tankards. The lights in the inn made her realise how dark it was.

Just around the bend was Hammersmith Terrace, where the house they were looking for was located.

Tall, narrow brick houses, typical of last century's buildings in London, with long yards which ran down to the Thames, but no front yards. Their doors opened onto a landing with one shallow step down to the road.

The smell from the river was more of a stench. August in London.

At a tap from Endellion, Jim stopped the carriage a few doors before they got to the house. She could see it. A faint light came through the shutters. They were in there.

Felix stowed his pistol in his driving coat pocket, and reached for the door. No. She *wasn't* going to be left behind again.

"You can't just knock on the door," Melissa said. "They won't answer, or they'll close it in your face."

"We could come at it from behind." Endellion indicated a laneway at the start of the block which headed towards the river.

"No time. I'll go in."

They both started arguing, but she wasn't going to listen.

"I'm *beautiful*," she said loudly. That shut them up. Endellion's mouth twitched with laughter, but she was serious. "Men have an odd reaction to me. When they meet me for the first time, they…they freeze. Just for a moment."

"That's true," Felix said. "Even some of my friends have."

"So *I'll* knock on the door. You two can be either side of it, and push in after me."

It was a good plan, and they knew it. They didn't like it, however.

"These are desperate men."

She shook her head. "No. They're not desperate. They think they've bamboozled everyone. They're probably quite pleased with themselves and relaxing in between torturing Charles." Her voice cracked on the last phrase and Argos whined and climbed into her lap.

"I'll take Argos," she added. Admittedly, a water spaniel wasn't the fiercest of dogs, but what better than a dog to allay suspicion?

The two men exchanged glances full of meaning, and then Endellion sighed.

"You don't knock until we're in position."

"Agreed."

A KNOCK AT THE DOOR.

Dark Hair got up and went to open it, saying, "About time you got back."

A light voice answered him.

"Is Augustine here yet?"

Melissa. That was Melissa's voice. Frantically, he sawed at the rope, not caring when he stabbed his wrist with each thrust.

"I'll come in and wait." She had the absolute authority of the aristocracy in her voice, and the man was stunned by her. No wonder. She appeared like a vision, floating in the door, pushing Dark Hair back, her dog at her heels like Artemis out hunting.

Dark Hair came to his senses as the last strand parted. He grabbed Melissa by the arm. Rage overtook Charles. He grabbed the chair, took two paces, and smashed it over the man's head while Argos bit into his calf.

He fell like a tree, and Charles kicked him in the gut, for good measure. Argos worried at the man's leg until Melissa called him off without looking away from Charles, her eyes shining.

Endellion Trengrouse stood in the doorway, pistol in hand. But outside a voice was raised.

"Oi! What're you doin–"

Fair Hair hurtled through the doorway

and landed on the floor, a jug of ale cracking as it fell from his hand, a stone bottle bouncing.

Felix came after him, shutting the door behind him, and pulled out a pistol as well.

Both heavies froze.

"Over by the wall," Felix said. His voice was pleasant enough, but the look on his face made them obey.

Charles turned to Melissa. "How—what…..?"

She smiled up at him, radiant, and then noticed his injuries. "Oh, Charles!"

"I'm fine."

"I'm very glad to hear that." A voice from the other end of the long room. They all spun, Endellion with pistol out while Felix kept his on the two men.

A man walked out of the gloom.

Leigh. Joshua Leigh. The traitor was a *member of Parliament*. Despicable. Charles pushed down the desire to grab a pistol and shoot him out of hand.

"Really, there was no reason for all this

brouhaha," Leigh said smoothly. "All I wanted was a chance to speak to you privately."

He looked meaningfully at the three Trengrouses, but Melissa shook her head.

"Augustine, I suppose. We stay for whatever discussion you need to have with Charles."

"They don't even know who you are," Charles said. "They don't mix with commoners."

Leigh flinched. "I wouldn't *be* a commoner if my grandfather hadn't stood on his bloody principles and refused to recant his faith. They stripped him of his title. With the Catholic Emancipation Bill, I could reclaim my seat in the Lords."

"This is all about Catholicism, Leigh? You've turned traitor to your king and country because the politics is going too slowly for you?"

Was the man mad?

Leigh smiled slowly. "Not *just* that. My mother is French. She's done quite well under Bonaparte. She is—was—a member of his court."

"How on Earth did you conceal that from the Foreign Office?"

"My dear boy, Castlereagh has no idea who I am. As far as anyone in this country knows, my mother is as dead as my father."

Charles felt anger grow, along with disgust. Men had died because this little twerp wanted to be a lord. Wanted *money.*

He opened his mouth to tell Felix to shoot the bastard.

CHARLES WAS ALIVE! Hurt, but only a little. Some cuts. Joy and relief almost overwhelmed her, bubbling up from stomach to chest to throat, wild and insistent, taking her over. She hadn't realised that happiness could make her mind buzz as much as anxiety did. A breath. Another.

Then a stranger walked in and started to gabble on. She had to concentrate. Joy could come later. She listened as they spoke, and took Endellion's handkerchief to bind up Charles' wrist.

So…Augustine was Mr Leigh. She knew that name. An MP, one who had worked with Charles before, although not someone she had met.

He had *not* planned to torture Charles, that was clear. Or, if he had, he'd changed his plans when he saw the situation.

Charles only rarely showed anger; usually when soldiers' lives had been thrown away by generals in search of glory. He was angry now, very angry.

She had to say something before he took action which would not be in his best interests.

"What do you want?" she asked.

"I *want* many things. For example, I *want* to know how you found this house."

As if she would boast about her cleverness. That was a weakness of Mr Leigh's, perhaps: *he* would want the glory, so he thought he could tempt the decoder to show "his" hand. She didn't understand normal social actions, but villainy was surprisingly easy to predict. She made a note of that for later.

"I'm sure you do." She looked him up and down, using every trick her mother had taught her for depressing pretension. He stiffened under her gaze. "What did you bring Charles to this place to hear?"

He looked at Endellion and Felix, but they stayed stalwart. He lowered his voice so the men on the floor couldn't eavesdrop.

"I felt, now Bonaparte has been decisively trounced, that I might change sides."

"You traitorous dog!"

Yes, Charles was angry. But he'd also be disappointed later, if he failed to capitalise on this situation.

"What can you offer?" Melissa kept her voice calm, to help Charles regain his balance.

"Why are you even *speaking*, girl?" Leigh sneered at her.

Charles hit him across the mouth. "And don't think I shall give you satisfaction for that, because I still owe you a few from those louts. You will speak to this lady with respect and a civil tone, or I will personally haul you to Bow Street and have you committed for treason."

"You have no proof. I plan to lease this house. That's why I have the keys. I came via the river this evening to inspect it, and found you and these ruffians… you have no evidence against me."

"I'm fairly sure these two will turn King's Evidence to avoid the noose," Felix said.

"I will and all!" Fair Hair piped up.

"Damn right!" Dark Hair growled. "We're not swinging for no gentry."

"And I imagine," Melissa added, "that there is considerable evidence at your home."

Silence fell.

"There *is* evidence," Leigh admitted. "And information." He wiped away a trickle of blood from his nose and seemed to gather himself. "Quite a lot of valuable information, and more where that came from."

Melissa let out a breath.

There it was. An offer too good to refuse. Did Charles see that?

"YOU WANT to turn informer on your employers?" Charles used the term deliberately, just to see Leigh's reaction.

"They are *not* my employers!" Oh, yes, there it was. His weakness. Pride. Still thinking of himself as an aristocrat, generations after it was true. That could be useful, later.

"Your…benefactors, then."

"We had mutual goals. Those goals are now unattainable, and it's time to…to reassess."

What a damned slimy coward!

This was what he had to look forward to in Vienna. Dealing with two-faced weasels like this. For the greater good.

"Yes," he said. "We have plenty of time to discuss this. People are accustomed to seeing us plan for Parliament together. This discussion doesn't have to happen tonight."

And the only reason it *was* happening tonight was that Leigh had planned to kill him and dump him in the river if his overtures hadn't been successful.

"I will require…compensation," Leigh said.

"You'll be getting compensation from your former masters, even if it's no longer from Bonaparte," Charles said. "For the moment, your compensation from Britain is that you are alive, and likely to remain so as long as you are honest with me."

Leigh pursed his mouth, but then nodded.

"And," Melissa added, "you will stay here, under my brothers' eyes, while Charles takes a note to your house and collects this information you say you have." She was magnificent. Always seeing every opportunity.

"That's evidence against me!" Leigh protested.

"Yes."

Charles grinned. "You heard the lady,

Leigh. I'm sure we can find paper and pen somewhere."

Felix produced an ivory notebook from his inside pocket, along with a pencil. "I use it for my calculations," he explained. Of course, he was an engineer.

"I'll go," Endellion said. "You can't walk in there looking like that, Charles, and I have a good idea of what to look for. Where's the safe?"

Sulkily, Leigh sat at the table and wrote out a note. "I don't have a safe. First thing people look for. The papers are in my gun case. There's a false bottom in the second drawer."

Endellion took the note, gave Charles his pistol, and went out.

Melissa was becoming calmer. Charles was all right, although the louts had treated him harshly. This should all work out well. Endellion was imposing—so tall, and broad with it. He could handle any recalcitrance at

Leigh's house, and he'd have Jim and Jim's offsider with him.

"What about these two?" Felix asked, gesturing the pistol towards the hectors. "Should I call up the watch?"

"What for?" Melissa asked. "Nothing illegal has happened here tonight."

Felix stared at her so blankly that Charles laughed.

"I'm afraid she's right, Felix. Nothing at *all* has happened tonight."

It took a moment for his meaning to sink in, and then Felix grimaced. "This is an ugly business you're in, Charles."

"It is," she agreed. "Necessary, however."

Charles looked the men over. At least he'd given Dark Hair back a bit of his own. "If I hear any whisper of what happened here, you'll both be hanged as traitors."

"Not us, m'lord! Silent as the grave," Dark Hair said.

If he asked for their names, they'd lie. He could always find them again through Leigh, if he needed to. He raised his chin at Felix, who nodded and moved his pistol to cover Leigh. The two men scrambled up and made for the door, slamming it behind them.

THAT MAN SHOULD NOT SIT down while Charles was injured. Melissa made Leigh sit on the floor so she could wash Charles' face with water from the kitchen pump. She did hope it didn't come straight from the Thames. His other injuries, he assured her, were mostly bruises.

After hearing Felix's account of the day, Charles took his pistol and sent him to the corner of the street to head off Luke Forester and his troopers, who would surely be coming soon.

Then they just sat, waiting for Endellion. Time seemed to stretch uncomfortably. She scratched under Argos's chin and he thumped his tail on the floor. Dear, faithful Argos.

Charles wouldn't meet her gaze. Had she done the wrong thing, coming here?

He hadn't been in danger after all. All her worry had been for nothing. That familiar feeling of getting everything wrong rose from her gut, flooding her with embarrassed heat.

"I'm sorry if I did the wrong thing…" she began. He reached out for her hand.

"No, no, my dear! You did *exactly* right, as you always do." He cast an exasperated look at Leigh. "We can't talk here."

"Then let me go," Leigh said immediately. "That man-mountain of yours must have what he wants by now."

Charles, wincing at bruised knuckles, fished his pocket-watch out and checked the time. "That's true. He's probably on his way back. But I'm not happy letting you go until we have solid evidence in our hand. Come on with you. I'm tired of holding this pistol."

He dragged Leigh up and took him to the kitchen pantry, slamming the door after him and wedging a chair against lst it.

Melissa smiled at him. She had done exactly right. That was all that mattered.

. . .

THEY WENT BACK into the main room, but Charles pulled the chair over so they could see the pantry door from where they sat.

He went behind it to offer her a seat, as if they were at a ball, but then looked her in the eyes before she could sit.

"I owe you an apology." He pulled at his neckcloth. Was it too tight? No, he was uncomfortable in a different way.

"Do you?" She couldn't think why.

Slowly, he came around the chair to stand in front of her. "When you...when you suggested marriage..."

Oh. That.

"No, I know I was wrong, it was silly of me, I shouldn't have–"

He put a finger on her lips. "It wasn't silly. It was a–a magnificent idea. I reacted as I did because–" He took a deep breath and let it out in a rush, then took another. Was he upset with her? How she wished she could read people's faces as Demelza did!

Charles ran a hand through his hair. "I can't marry you because I'm not good enough for you."

Her stomach was churning and she felt vaguely angry. Why was he being so *stupid*? "That is ridiculous."

"No." He turned away, but then turned back. "I can't give you a normal married life, Melissa. No matter how much I love you."

"You love me?" There was that fountain of joy again. How odd. She'd never *wanted* to be loved, but if it was Charles…that made all the difference.

CHAPTER 10

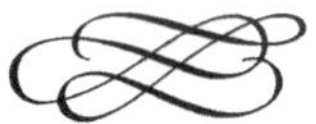

Her face was alight at his confession of love, but Charles knew he had to quench that light.

"So much. But I'm not made like other men, Melissa. I can't...I can't give you children. I can't even–" He hesitated, glancing down at his feet and then forced himself to look up. He could feel a blush staining his cheeks. "I can't even give you marital relations. I just...I just don't seem to *desire* anyone. Not women or men. Not even you. You're *so* beautiful, and yet– I shouldn't have reacted as I did at the ball. I'm sorry to the bottom of my heart that I just refused you without an explanation."

Slowly, so slowly, Melissa smiled. Not just a smile: her whole face was alive and happy and radiant. What on Earth–

"No children?" He shook his head. Her smiled broadened.

"No marital relations?" He bit his lip and shook it again. A terrible admission to make. He'd always known he wasn't much of a man, but to have to confess it to Melissa cut into his soul.

"But that's *wonderful!*"

What?

She did a little dance around the room, and came back to him, while he stood there like a numbskull.

"Is it really true? What about an heir? Do you need an heir?"

He shook his head. "No. I have a cousin…not that there's much to inherit, except the title. I've never expected to sire an heir."

She danced again, reaching for his hands,

inviting him to match her steps. Her face never lost its radiance.

"*Not* have to have children! *Not* to have coitus! Oh, Charles, I'm so happy! I was *dreading*…but I was prepared to do it, if I *had* to, if you wanted it, just to have you as my husband."

His brain was working very slowly. She *didn't* want children? Or…anything else?

"Now we can be happy together!"

He began to dance too, the steps of a quadrille—a little odd without the other couple facing them, but it didn't matter. Why had he ever thought Melissa would be like other women? Of course she wasn't!

He should have known that they were perfectly suited in every way.

CHARLES HAD LOST that haunted look. His eyes were bright. He began to dance, and then stopped. He held her hands and went down on one knee. He was going to propose! But he didn't have to—she'd already done that. Perhaps it was one of those social rules she'd never understand.

Argos left her side, put his front paws on Charles' knee and licked his face.

They both laughed, a little giddy. How appropriate that Charles had Argos as his second.

"Lady Melissa, would you do me the very great honour of becoming my wife?"

She grinned at him, so happy it burst out of her.

"Of course I will!"

Would he try to kiss her? Or had he meant that he wanted *none* of the things men and women did together? She didn't like the idea of kissing, but if it were Charles…

He rose and took a step towards her, Argos rubbing his head against her knee.

Not a kiss. Charles pulled her into an embrace. A hug.

Oh.

He was so big and warm. This wasn't the repulsive pawing she had been subject to in the past.

This was like being at the bottom of a pile of puppies. Warm, and strong, and safe.

She slid her arms around him and basked in the feeling. The buzzing joy turned to comforting, warm happiness.

She and Charles. It would all be all right now.

HOW LOVELY IT was to hold her, knowing she expected nothing more! A peace he'd never felt filled him. Melissa loved him just as he was. Was happy *because* he was as he was. Was there any greater blessing?

Charles pulled back and looked her in the eyes. There was one more thing.

"There's just one thing…Castlereagh has offered me an attaché's position in Vienna. The Prime Minister is pulling all his agents in. Collapsing the network of informants."

"That seems very short-sighted." He laughed. His own words to Castlereagh. They thought as one.

"It is. Which is why Castlereagh wants his

own men in key locations. Would you…do you think you might like to live in Vienna?"

He didn't *need* the job in Vienna any more…but he didn't want to live off Melissa's money. Besides, it would be interesting, to be part of the rebuilding of Europe.

"Vienna was a Roman settlement," she said thoughtfully. "I'm sure I could find research there to occupy my time. And there are some monasteries nearby which have some fascinating manuscripts in their libraries."

That was his Melissa. He was quite interested in those manuscripts too.

Endellion came through the door. His instinct was to spring apart, but they didn't have to. Not now.

Endellion took one look at them and grinned. "About time." He brandished a sheaf of papers. "I have enough here to hang Leigh ten times over. There were false bottoms in *several* drawers."

Reluctantly, Charles let Melissa go. "Excellent."

They went to the pantry and let Leigh out.

"Off you go, then," Charles said. "I'll call on you tomorrow and we can plan how this will work."

Looking decidedly ruffled, Leigh took himself out the back door. Good riddance.

THE THREE OF THEM, Argos bounding ahead, went to the front. Melissa wasn't sure what she should do now.

"I have to report all this to the Foreign Office and send a dispatch to Castlereagh through the diplomatic pouch," Charles said with reluctance.

Of course he did. But there was a solution which didn't involve waking up the servants in the Trengrouse townhouse. "I'll go with Endellion—I can stay at your house, can't I?"

"Naturally."

"Tomorrow, I can take you home, and talk to your parents about our marriage,"

Charles said. "Ideally, we can get it done before I leave for Vienna."

"I'll buy you a special licence as a wedding present." Endellion grinned at her. "It might be a bit much to expect our uncle the bishop to perform *two* hasty marriages in the space of a week!"

Charles slapped him on the shoulder. "I'll accept with thanks. At least I know your father will give his approval."

"Been on at you, has he? Not surprised. You were dragging your feet a tad." Endellion looked at both of them, his gaze seeming wistful. "I'm very glad you have found your way to one another. I think I don't need to wish you happy: you'll be fine without that."

He went into the street to call the carriage to them. Poor Jim. What a long day and night this had been for him.

A thought struck her.

"You know, Charles, Vienna would be an excellent, central place from which to run a network of informants."

He gave a shout of laughter. "So I told

Castlereagh!" He smiled down at her. "You, my dear, are the perfect woman for me."

For the first time in her life, she was what she should be. It was an odd, dizzying feeling. To be valued completely for who she was. Just as she was. She could feel herself expanding, as though it was all right for her now to take up more space.

She smiled up at Charles.

"And you are the perfect man for me. My earl, the spy."

Argos barked as if agreeing, and they both laughed as they went down the step to the footpath, together.

They were walking into their future, Melissa thought. A future which held so much more than she had dared imagine.

EPILOGUE

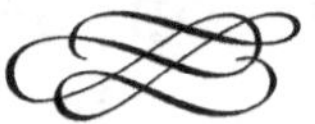

VIENNA

Crystal and silver sparkled in the light of fifty wax candles. The scent of pine garlands strung around the dining-room fireplace wafted to the guests and mixed with the rich aroma of claret, being served with the beef course.

Yes. Good.

Melissa nodded as an elderly Italian conte, sitting at her right hand, began to describe the wonders of Firenze.

Everyone was here and in their correct places. Luke Forester—a civilian now, pretending to be an idle young man doing a belated Grand Tour—sat across from the young count who was the focus of this dinner. Luke would 'befriend' him. The man held a sinecure in Metternich's office; he barely attended his workplace, but he had access to invaluable gossip.

Frau Hemming was between a British colonel and a French bishop. She was Melissa's charge for the evening. Nothing important yet. But, as she'd pointed out to Charles, women knew far more than their husbands or fathers believed, and they talked to one another. Madeleine Hemming was married to an Austrian colonel, and just knowing when her husband was out of town would be helpful. Small pieces of information, put together by someone who saw the big picture, could change the fate of nations.

Melissa had established that *her* dinners would be held *'en famille'*, with small numbers and guests encouraged to speak across the table instead of keeping to the strict formula of only speaking to the people on either side, during alternate courses.

"They will speak more freely in such an atmosphere," she'd told Charles. Besides, it meant she could keep Argos next to her chair with only a few raised eyebrows from their guests.

She was pleased to see that she'd been right. Since everyone spoke French, the language of diplomacy, there were no barriers to understanding. Conversations ebbed and flowed naturally, and the atmosphere relaxed as the meal went on.

The murmur of voices, the discreet clattering of cutlery on plates, the bright lights… in the past, this would have been torture. Not now. Tonight had a *purpose*, unlike all the other dinners. She and Charles, and their people, working together.

Social gatherings were no longer torment when one had a reason for being there. It was exhilarating.

After all, she'd been pretending to be like

other people all her life. At least now it was *useful*. She was where she needed to be, using all the skills her mother had so diligently schooled her in, working for King and Country. And for Charles, who made her so happy. She smiled up the table at him.

MELISSA HAD ENCHANTED EVERYONE, of course. The old conte was droning on as he always did, but his eyes were bright and he would no doubt say more than he intended. She would remember every word, and after they guests had gone, they would take Argos for a walk, and talk over everything that happened, and make plans. Equal partners in their work, no matter how it seemed to the world.

What had he done to deserve this luck? This *blessing*.

Colonel Hemming made a comment about the new production of *The Magic Flute* at the Kärntnertortheater. Pulling his attention back, Charles noted it was a shame they had missed last year's production of Beethoven's *Fidelio,* which caused a general discussion amongst those who had seen it.

"What an excellent hostess your wife is," the colonel said. "Dining *en famille* is so pleasant. So homely."

"It suits us," Charles said. Melissa smiled at him and Charles toasted her silently.

The perfect woman for him.

MORE BY ELIZABETH LEYDIN

I hope you've enjoyed the fifth book in the Trengrouse Ball series. There are more–see below.

Sign up for Elizabeth's Substack blog, 'Corsets & Coaches', where she shares true-life Regency stories and tidbits, as well as news about her latest releases, or watch her "This Week in the Regency" videos on Youtube.

More Trengrouse Ball Sweet Regency Romances

The Trengrouse Ball books can all be read as stand-alones – the timelines overlap, but each story is separate.

The Captain & The Lady
Book 1 in The Trengrouse Ball series

Petroc Trengrouse has come home from Waterloo missing his right leg. Family friend Lady Beatrice Marlowe has been thrown out of her home on the deaths of her father and brother.

When Petroc comes to stay at Beatrice's mother's seaside house to recover from his wounds, he has no idea that he's causing severe financial problems.

He feels he's not fit to marry; she knows she's too poor to attract an aristocratic suitor. Will the Trengrouse Ball prove both of them wrong?

The Youngest Son
Book 2 in the Trengrouse Ball series

When Ives Trengrouse hijacks his friend Den's coach after the Trengrouse Ball, he thinks it's only a prank. But Den isn't inside. Instead, it's his sister Katie, going home early with a migraine.

Compromised beyond saving, the two must marry immediately—and do so. Katie's dreams of a big London Season are gone. Ives can't go on his light-hearted, care-for-nothing way now he's a married man.

Neither of them wants to be in this marriage: can they turn childhood friendship into something deeper?

Second Chance at Christmas
Book 3 in the Trengrouse Ball series

A heart-warming second chance Christmas story.

Widowed, pregnant Lady Demelza Mandeville returns to her family home, Trengrouse Hall, after her husband's recent death, dreading meeting family friend, Sir Denzell Kelynack, who jilted her in her first Season.

Denzell looks forward to the meeting—he wants to know why Demelza had jilted him eight years ago. And what role did his needy, unstable mother play in that?

Finding out the truth, and finding a path to a new life, is complicated by Demelza's pregnancy. If the baby is a boy, she'll be bound to the Mandeville estates until he's an adult; if a girl, she's free to live her own life while a Mandeville cousin inherits the estate.

The Trengrouse Ball is a promise of things to come, but will the promise come true at Christmas?

The Baboon at the Ball
Book 4 in the Trengrouse Ball series

A forbidden love story with animal antics to upset the normal order of things! (Or, a Cinderella story with a difference…)

Val Muffet is a Cit—a rich, well-educated, beautifully-mannered man, but definitely *not* one of the *ton*, despite being invited to the Trengrouse Ball.

Lady Kerenza Trengrouse's family is amongst the great and the good of the land, and she expects to marry a lord. An earl, at least!

What could bring these two to care about each other? Enter Genevieve, the lost, forlorn but definitely challenging baboon, given to the Muffets by the Prince Regent himself.

Genevieve is *not* invited to the ball, but she comes anyway, and life will never be the same again for Val or Kerenza!

The Lion and Miss Lamb
Book 6 in the Trengrouse Ball series

Sarah Lamb doesn't have a family; Endellion Trengrouse has never fit in with his.

Immediately attracted, the two have a brief flirtation at the Trengrouse Ball, which ends disastrously when Endellion finds out the truth behind Sarah's birth. Sarah isn't surprised by his reaction: no respectable man will marry an illegitimate orphan.

But there's more to Sarah's parentage—and Endellion's—than either of them know. Can they find the truth…and will that truth bring them together, or drive them apart?